MY THANKSGIVING FAUX PAW

PECULIAR MYSTERIES BOOK 10

RENEE GEORGE

BARKSIDE OF THE MOON PRESS

My Thanksgiving Faux Paw

Peculiar Mysteries Book 10

Copyright © 2019 by Renee George

Publisher: Barkside of the Moon Press

Print ISBN: 978-1-947177-33-8

For Mom.
I haven't always understood you,
but I always love you.
Thanks for believing in me.

ACKNOWLEDGMENTS

I have to thank my BFF sister Robbin Clubb, who was with me every step of the way, and BFF Michele Bardsley for her excellent notes and critiques! This one was an emotional journey for me, and I hope it translates for the readers!

To my Rebels, I love you guys more than you know! Thanks for always supporting me.

Oh! And lest I forget, thank you hot black coffee. I would be dead, or at least I'd get a full eight of hours sleep, without you.

For this secret shifter town in the Ozarks, holidays have never been normal...

Human psychic Sunny Haddock has everything she's ever wanted: a stable home, a loving husband, two kids, and great friends. Granted, everyone she knows (and has birthed) is on the furry side, but so what?

Weird is wonderful, especially in this wacky little place she calls home.

But when a young man shows up on her doorstep claiming to be her long lost brother, his presence provokes a psychic walk down memory lane, challenging Sunny's ideas about herself and her future. Throw in exploding turkeys, time-traveling visions, and good old-fashioned family drama... and you have a Thanksgiving that's gonna be downright Peculiar.

CHAPTER 1

Kablam!

Hoots and howls erupted from the men as they scuttled away from the metal cylinder sitting in the center of our backyard. One of those four yowling spouses belonged to me. Babe was the handsomest coyote shifter this side of the Ozarks. Even when he was red-faced and cursing.

"I tried to tell him," Chav Smith, my best friend, said to me, Willy Boden-Corman, and Ruth Thompson. We'd all gathered on the back porch to watch the show.

And man-oh-man, what a show.

The hoots and howls turned into shouts of alarm as flames shot ten feet into the air, spraying fire everywhere. Luckily, all the men had vacated the hot zone. Babe, Billy Bob, Brady, and Ed did a panicked dance around the fire, swatting at it with towels and stripped T-shirts.

"This is awesome," I said, watching our shirtless hotties turn pink in the heat. "Good call on that one, Chav."

"I'm no dummy," she said. Chav's mahogany colored hair was pulled back into a braid, something she did more regularly now that she had a newborn whose tiny hands could yank those glossy locks really hard. She fidgeted with the braid's brush-like tip and shook her head. "Deep frying a turkey has disaster written all over it."

Our shortest and sassiest pal, Willy, nibbled on her lower lip. "Um, not to take away any value from this Darwin award moment, but all the kids are in the house, right?" Willy asked. She and her husband had a two-year-old with Willy's red hair and Brady's golden-colored eyes.

"Yep," Ruth said distractedly. Her big brown eyes were wide with interest as her Disney princess nose twitched. "Lisa Ann and Mariah are playing with them in the living room." Lisa Ann and Mariah were the youngest Thompson girls and neither minded babysitting the little ones, especially since we were all paying them twenty dollars per child.

"Oh!" Willy said on a laugh.

Her husband Brady's T-shirt had burst into flames. He threw it down, and Babe and Ed took turns stomping on it.

"This is fascinating," I observed. "Do you think if we wait long enough, they'll take off their pants?"

Chav snorted. "As much as I love this new game of strip-so-you-don't-die, it's officially getting out of hand." She heaved up the fire extinguisher she'd brought from the kitchen.

"Spoil sport," I told her, frowning as she pulled the pin and walked toward the fire. It had started to die down already, and a directed spray at the center of the inferno put it the rest of the way out.

Willy, Ruth, and I enthusiastically clapped our approval. Chav did a quick curtsey in our direction.

Billy Bob and Ed put their slightly charred shirts back on. Babe's was toast, and so was Brady's, of course. I walked to Babe and slid my arms around his trim waist. The man had muscles on his muscles. Yummy. "I've heard of dinner and a show, but dinner as a show?"

"For the record," Chav said, "I told them twice that putting a frozen turkey into hot peanut oil was a seriously bad idea."

Babe grinned at his sister then gave me a kiss. "Do we have another turkey?"

"We have a tofurkey," I said. Since my visions, which focused mostly on animalkind, forced me to be a vegetarian, I'd bought the tofu turkey for myself.

Babe made a face. "Yuck."

I grunted. "If I had known you were going to turn the turkey into a weapon of mass destruction, I'd have bought a spare."

He playfully swatted my butt. "And here I thought I married a psychic."

I knew Babe was razzing me, but sometimes I wished my psychic ability worked better on the people I loved. Unfortunately, the more space someone took up in my heart the less space they took up in my visions. I snuggled closer, enjoying the warmth of his chest against my cheek. I tilted my head back to meet his gaze and wiggled my brows. "I have a few predictions for later."

"Oh yeah?"

"All right," Chav said. "How about we keep Thanksgiving festivities rated PG." She'd traded the fire extinguisher for the cutest little cuddle-monkey num-num in the whole wide world, my adorable nephew Rory.

I disengaged from Babe. "Give me that baby!" I held out my arms and made a silly face.

Rory kicked out his tiny legs and made a happy gasp.

Chav laughed as she handed him over. "All the noise out here woke him up from his nap." Rory was five-months-old with Chav's dark brown hair and Billy Bob's gray eyes.

Billy Bob wrapped his arms around Chav from behind. "Sorry we ruined Thanksgiving."

"It's not technically Thanksgiving," Willy said.

"Close enough," I told her. My BFFs and I had planned a big potluck get-together today, which was the Sunday before traditional Thanksgiving. And, as Ruth said when we were concocting our plan, "It's a good excuse to eat lots of pie."

I personally didn't need a "good excuse" to eat pie. A day ending in "y" was a reason enough for me. "Besides, it's not ruined," I said to Rory as I nibbled his yummy toes. "Auntie Sunny also bought two spiral hams."

"And Mommy," Chav said, lightly booping her baby's nose, "brought an extra turkey." She tilted her head back to look at her husband. "It's in the cooler in the trunk."

"I'll get the oil going," Babe offered.

"You will not," I protested.

"It's already cooked," Chav said as she kidnapped her son straight from my unwilling arms. "No deep frying required."

"You're amazing," said Billie Bob. He leaned over to coo at Rory. "Isn't your mama amazing?"

"So, are you," Babe whispered to me. I turned in my husband's arms, so my back was to his front, and I wiggled my derriere against his groin. He growled his pleasure.

A vibration against my booty made me giggle. I elbowed Babe in the ribs. "Is that your phone or are you just happy to see me?"

He laughed. "Both." He dug into his pocket for his cell phone and glanced at the screen. "It's the sheriff. I better take it."

My husband was officially the Mayor of Peculiar now. He'd won the vote in a landslide victory. Of course, he'd been unopposed, so that made his campaign cheap and easy. Part of his responsibility, though, was taking calls from the sheriff even when he was off duty with his family.

"Hello," he said. His brow furrowed, creating the cutest little groove between his eyes. He frowned. "Who?"

I mouthed the words, "What's going on?"

Babe held up a give-me-a-moment finger. "Repeat that." He nodded. "Okay. I'll ask." Babe took the phone from his ear and looked at me. "Do you know a Jonathan William Haddock?"

"Never heard of him." But the fact that his last name was Haddock raised more than a few alarm bells. "Who is he?"

Babe widened his eyes. "He claims to be your brother."

"I don't have a brother," I said.

Babe put the phone back to his ear. "Sunny says she

doesn't have a brother. Uh-huh. Yep. Okay. Hold on." Babe took the phone from his ear again. "The guy says his parents are Jerry and Rhonda Haddock."

I frowned. "Those are my parents' names. How old is he?".

"Twenty," Babe replied. When I raised a brow, he said, "Sheriff heard your question."

Sheriff Sid Taylor was a raccoon shifter, and like all the therians in Peculiar, had really good hearing.

I shook my head. "This is a joke, right? I mean, it's November, but it's feeling a lot like April Fool's."

Babe gave me a sympathetic frown. "The sheriff wants to bring him to the house."

I narrowed my eyes. "Do you really think bringing a human to our fur-filled pre-Thanksgiving extravaganza is a good idea?"

Babe shrugged. "Sheriff says he can't stay in town."

"But my party." I gestured to the scorched earth. "It's just getting started."

"I say the more the merrier," Ruth interjected with a little too much perk.

"Traitor," I said.

"I think we can all control ourselves long enough to meet this brother of yours," Willy added.

I shook my head emphatically as a coyote pup with superhero underwear sliding down his hind legs ran between us. "Can we?" I asked. "Can we all control ourselves?" The pup headed into the woods. I frowned at my husband. "Go get your son before he makes it to town."

"Oh, he's my son now," he said.

"When he's all furry and running around on four paws?" I gently poked his chest and winked. "You betcha."

Babe's low chuckle made me shiver with pleasure. He grabbed me around the waist and yanked me close, cupping my neck as he kissed me until my toes curled backwards. "I'll go get my son," he said. "You get the house human safe for when your brother arrives."

By the time I got my bearings, Babe was already hot-footing it into the woods. "I don't have a brother!" I yelled at him.

"Maybe we should all try this next weekend," Brady said.

"Oh, hell no," Willy told her husband. "I ain't leaving until I see this Jonathan William Haddock for myself."

"See. That name alone should tell you he's not my brother. If my parents had given birth to him his name would be something like Sagittarius Moonbeam."

"Come on, your parents can't be that weird," Willy said.

"Hello. These would be the same people who named me Ambrosia Sunshine."

"Good point." The fiery redhead crossed her arms, her stance daring me or anyone else to tell her to leave. "Even so, I'm staying until the alleged baby bro arrives."

Chav nodded. "If Willy is staying, then Doc and I have to stay. You know, in case any medical attention is required."

I glared at her. "Do you think this guy is bringing a shotgun?"

"I'm not talking about a doctor for you," said Chav.

"Once you're done with him, your brother might need a Band-aid or two."

"Hah! For the last time, I don't have a brother. No siblings. *None.* My mom was older than dirt when I left their whack-a-doodle cult. Too old to have any more babies."

"How old?" Ruth asked.

I paused. My mom had been thirty-seven when I'd left. Younger than I was right now, and I'd had two babies over the past five years. I let loose a defeated sigh. "Okay. She could've had another kid." I felt my stomach squeeze with dread. It never occurred to me that Jerry and Rhonda would make another baby. After all, I'd barely been eighteen when I left and I figured they'd be happy to be rid of me. I always felt like a burden—when I wasn't feeling like their show pony. "I haven't talked to them since I left the commune."

Chav and Ruth shared a look. "Not at all?" asked Ruth, her voice soft with empathy.

"They tried. I got letters every now and then. A few phone calls. But I'd already had eighteen years of their weird cultish ways."

"How did they find you?" asked Chav.

"I don't know. Or care."

"Besides, you got us now," said Willie. "And we won't let anyone hurt you."

"We have shovels," added Ruth.

"And a whole lot of woods where no one will every find a body."

I sniffed. "You must really love me. Aw. Okay, okay.

You can stay. But we need to do something with the kids. They change at a whim these days, and unless you can figure out how to explain to a bunch of small children and babies that they can't go furry around the human, they can't be here when this Jonathan dude arrives."

Babe trotted out of the woods holding our back-to-biped, naked, giggling son upside down by his ankles, his one-eyed winky wagging at all of us like a puppy tail.

"Where is his underwear?" I asked.

"Out in the woods somewhere." Babe flipped Jude over, and our son laughed with so much joy as he landed on his feet and sprinted toward the house.

"Are you sure that kid don't have cat in him?" Willy asked.

She was a cougar shifter, so I got the joke, but I was too stressed out to laugh. "How are we supposed to keep the kids from shifting when Jonathan gets here? It's an impossible situation. Call Sid and tell him that he can't bring him."

Ed stepped up. "How about if the dads take the kids to the park? Linus and the girls can help us keep them corralled." Linus was Ruth and Ed's youngest son. "You text us when the coast is clear."

Babe, Billy Bob, and Brady glanced at each other, and then nodded their agreement.

"Sounds like a plan," Babe said.

"No way, mister," I told my big hunka-burnin'-coyote. "You stay."

"And the kids?"

I frowned. "They can go."

"Do you want us to go?" Chav asked.

"Noooo." Willy groaned her dissent.

"You three to stay," I said. "I need the BFF brigade for support."

Ruth looped her arm in mine. "Then we stay."

Willy snorted. "Like we were going to leave."

CHAPTER 2

By the time Sheriff Taylor pulled into our driveway, the dads, minus Babe, had somehow managed to gather up all the children and escape.

Chav smacked my hand. "Get your fingernail out of your mouth."

"Uhhhng," I whined. "I can't help it."

Sheriff Taylor got out first then opened the back door of his patrol car.

"Poor guy," Ruth said as a nice-looking young man slid out and stood up. He had brown hair, the color of mine before I met Miss Clairol, and he was wearing jeans, a tan bomber jacket, and a pair of blue canvas shoes.

"Nope. That is no child of Jerry and Rhonda Haddock." I waved my hand. "Too normal."

Babe rubbed my shoulders. "You got this."

When the young man locked gazes with me, I recognized my dad in the slight downturn at the outer edges of his eyes. It had been so long since I'd seen my father, the resemblance hit me harder than I expected. My lower lip started to tremble.

Babe massaged harder.

"I'm okay," I squeaked out. I put my hands over his before he wore holes in my muscles.

"Babe," the sheriff said when they approached the porch. "Sunny."

"Hey, Sid," I said.

He presented the newcomer. "This is Jonathan Haddock."

"Jack," the young man said. Even though he was on the thin side, and not overly tall, maybe five-feet-eleven inches, his voice was a deep baritone. "Wow." He shuffled nervously. "Mom and Dad had some pictures from when you were young. Except for your hair color, you haven't changed much."

"Mom and Dad, huh?" I narrowed my gaze. I never got to call them Mom and Dad. They insisted on me using their first names because "parental monikers are manacles of the patriarchy."

Jack held his hand out to me. "It's nice to finally meet you."

I felt my expression sour, but I took his hand for a quick shake. "Yeah, you too."

He laughed, and it sounded like my mom's laugh. Hurt that I hadn't expected to feel twisted in my stomach.

"You don't believe a word I'm saying do you?"

"Nope."

"I'm telling you the truth. You're my sister."

"Uh-huh. And you're showing up out of the blue because…"

"I came to warn you."

"Warn her about what?" Babe asked. He moved from behind me to create a semi-barrier between me and Jack. My husband stands at six feet five inches, an intimidating height, even among therians.

Jack put up his hands. "Not from me," he said. He narrowed his eyes at me. "This is going to sound weird and hard to believe, but I'm psychic."

My friends, the sheriff, and my husband all chuckled.

Jack sighed. "I get that reaction a lot."

This young man was telling me he was the child of my parents *and* he was psychic? I decided to test him. "Sure, you're a psychic, and I'm a shapeshifter." I waved my arms with great exaggeration. "As a matter of fact, we're all shapeshifters."

To the credit of my therianthrope friends and family, none of them reacted.

Jack frowned. "I'm not lying."

Neither was I, but he didn't need to know that. "Prove it."

"Can I touch you? Your hand will do."

I stepped down from the porch and held out my hand.

"Nope," said Chav. She pulled me back. "Do me." She glanced back. "If he knows your parents, even if he isn't your brother, he might have information to read you with, but he doesn't know me."

I nodded. "Okay. Be careful."

"I'm not planning anything dangerous," Jack said.

"Better not be," I told him. "I'd hate for Chav to have to eat you for dinner." I'd seen her, in her gigantic Brother

Wolf form, eat a whole serial killer. I chuckled like I was kidding, and everyone let out pensive breaths.

Chavvah held her hand out to the newcomer. "Just let the man do his thing."

Jack stretched his fingers toward Chav's palm. He flinched when his skin made contact with hers. If he was psychic, I could only guess at what her mojo as a spirit talker was doing to his mind.

"Close your eyes and think of a happy memory," Jack said. "One that you really connect with."

"Why happy?" Chav asked.

"Those are the most pleasant ones to live through." He smiled. "But try to pick something you wouldn't mind a stranger seeing."

Chav looked back at me, her frown matching my own. Then she shrugged. "No problem." She closed her eyes.

Jack's body jerked. His head flew back. He jerked again--his entire body animated except for the fingertip touching Chav's palm. Sid and Babe surged toward them, but Jack stilled.

"Don't," I said. "He's not hurting her. Look. He's barely touching her."

"Sunny, I've been privy to your kind of strange for a while now, but this is cuckoo even by your standards," Sid said.

"I agree with Sunny," Willy said. "Let it play out. I don't think Chav's, uhm, brother, and I'm not talking about Babe here, will let anything happen to his girl." Willy was talking about Chav's spirit guide, Brother Wolf. He had a protective streak when it came to my BFF.

"Sid has a point," Ruth interjected. "This is bizarre."

Nothing happened. Nada. Zip. Jack let go of Chav's hand and smiled as if to say, "Ta da!"

"Well?" I asked, less than impressed by the self-proclaimed Zoltar. "Will she fall in love? Will she win the lottery? Get that job she's been pining for?"

Jack grinned. "You're funny."

I crossed my arms over my chest. "And you've got about two seconds before I have the Sheriff here put you back into his patrol car and drive you to the next town."

Jack winked at me. *Winked!* The little shit. Then he turned to Chav and said, "Your wedding, just as the sun set and the moon rose over the lake was really beautiful. Thank you for taking me on that journey with you." He rubbed his shoulder. "The pre-wedding fight with your step-daughter was unusual, though."

Chav's eyes widened.

Everyone took a step back from Jack, putting distance between their bodies and his hands.

"It's a family tradition. It's good luck to fight on the wedding day, with, erm, family." I grimaced at my lie, but I was committed now. "I bet folks in northern California have wedding rituals that people around here would find different."

"They might." He frowned. "But I wouldn't know. I grew up in Arkansas."

"Really? They moved the commune to Arkansas." Maybe Arkansas offered big tax breaks for "religious" communities. Even so, from what I knew of the state, it had some fairly conservative leanings. "Weird."

"No commune, Sunny."

"Then you can't be my brother. My parents were dedicated to the Zen-wiccan-druidic-Hindu and whatever other philosophy or religion that suited their day to day cult-y whims."

"I know it's been a long time, but I swear, they don't belong to a cult. Dad's an accountant. Mom's a kindergarten teacher."

"A-ha!" I pointed at him. "Jerry and Rhonda are pot farmers."

His brows furrowed in consternation. "Mom and Dad are the most strait-laced people I know. They didn't tell me much about their past before Arkansas, but whatever they did before I was born, they left it all behind after." He narrowed his gaze on me, his voice lowering to conspiracy levels. "They really grew marijuana?"

"They grew it, picked it, rolled it, and smoked it," I said.

Jack guffawed. "I can't wait to bring this up at Thanksgiving dinner." He clapped his hands together. "So much to be thankful for."

An aching twinge of jealousy pinched my gut. We'd never celebrated an intimate Thanksgiving as a family when I was growing up. Instead, the commune would commemorate a community wide harvest festival, complete with dried corn gathering, compost mixing, and other crappy activities, like using corn husks for basket weaving. I rarely saw my parents during the events.

Ruth, who always seemed to know the right thing to say, said, "Well, since the whole psychic thing seems to be true, maybe we should all go inside and have a chat over pie."

"I never say no to pie," Jack said.

Willy put her hand on my shoulder. "You guys are definitely related."

I rolled my eyes. "Liking pie is not a genetic trait."

Chav stopped me from going into the house. "You all go ahead. We'll be right in."

Sid tipped his hat. "I'm off. Call me if you need me to escort this young man out of town."

We waved at the sheriff as he pulled out of the drive, but Chav's deep frown lines worried me. "What is it?" I asked when we were finally alone.

"I relived my wedding," she said.

"You mean you were thinking about it, right?"

"No. I actually relived it. It was like I was there for the entire day from the end of the fight until the *I do's*. I could feel, smell, taste, and hear everything as if I was experiencing it all over again."

"Really?" My visions mostly felt dreamlike. Real but distant. "So Jack somehow tapped into your memory?"

"More than a memory, Sunny. I was there." She shook her head. "But that's not the weirdest part."

"I'm afraid to ask."

"Jack was there." She rubbed the creases between her eyes. "I swear."

"In your mind, like a presence?"

"No," she said. "He was actually there. At my wedding."

CHAPTER 3

I'd put the two extra leaves into the dining room table the night before, so there was enough room to seat eight people. Ruth stood at the end, dishing up pecan and pumpkin pie. Jack sat on the right, Willy and Babe sat on the left.

My darling husband scowled at the young man. To Jack's credit, or maybe he was just too naïve to be scared, he happily dug into his pecan pie slice.

"This is stupid good," he told Ruth.

She glowed at the compliment. "I'm glad you like it. I have more if you're still hungry after that piece."

"I definitely want to try some of that pumpkin," Jack said, before spooning in another mouthful. "Mmm mmm."

"Making yourself at home?" I asked.

Jack's mouth tugged up at the corner in a sly smile, but he didn't stop chewing.

"Do you have any real proof that you're my brother?"

He swallowed. "Would a birth certificate do? I'd offer my blood, but a DNA test takes weeks."

"I supposed Jerry and Rhonda told you I was psychic, too. Right?"

"You're psychic?" He frowned. "Mom and Dad didn't tell me that."

"That surprises me. They liked to tell anyone who would listen at the commune. They used to parade me out like a show pony every time there was a party, and since the commune grew their own weed and shrooms, there were a lot of freaking parties. Did they send you to find me?"

"They don't know I'm here. They think I went to Grandpa Jasper's in Mountain Home."

"Who's Grandpa Jasper?"

He stared at me as if trying to decide if I was joking. "Dad's dad."

"Jerry's dad is deceased. So is his mother. Same with Rhonda's parents." I was told all my life that my parents didn't have any family beyond the commune.

"Grandma Evelyn and Grammy Sue would have a whole lot to say about that."

"Fascinating," Willy said, using her cop voice. "But this isn't an episode of Jerry Springer. Get to the point. Tell us why you've tracked Sunny down."

"Is it hot in here?" My lungs were tight, and I struggled to catch my breath. I couldn't wrap my head around Jerry and Rhonda having another kid and ditching their oh-so-important whack-a-doodle beliefs to give him a normal upbringing. On top of that, they'd lied to me about my relatives. When I'd run away from the commune at eighteen and moved to San Diego, I'd struggled for almost a year trying to find enough work to put a roof over my head.

Anger surged inside me. "I had to live in a homeless shelter for two months, working cash jobs because Jerry and Rhonda thought that government identification, like birth certificates and driver's licenses, were part of the patriarchal overreach." My voice grew louder and my words faster as I continued. "I couldn't get a real job without a social security number! They ruined my childhood and sabotaged my adulthood and for what? A belief system they tossed away for… for you?"

Babe had gotten up from his chair and he pulled me into a hug. "You don't have to do this right now, sweetheart."

"Now or later, it doesn't matter. I don't see this getting any easier."

"I'm really sorry," Jack said. "Mom and Dad don't talk much about their life before I was born. It's a sore spot for the family." He lowered his head and stared at his empty pie plate. "I didn't even know about you until recently."

Ouch. "Out of sight, out of mind," I told him.

"That's not it," Jack said. "I think it just hurt them to talk about you. At least, that's what they told me when I asked."

My brow lowered. "How did you know to ask? Did you get a vision from them about me?"

He shook his head and met my gaze. "No. I can't read them at all. Grammy Sue is a psychic, though her powers aren't nearly as developed as mine. She told me that her gift didn't work on people she loved. The more she was attached to someone, the less she could see of their destiny."

Hearing I had a grandmother who was psychic, and whose gift was similar to mine, made me sad and angry all at the same time. If I had known about her, maybe she could have helped me navigate some of the rougher periods of my life. "Does she know about me?"

He looked away and sighed. "I don't know. Maybe. But she never spoke about you to me."

"Then how did you find out about me?" I asked. It seemed that Rhonda and Jerry had done everything they could to forget they had a daughter at all. Hurt cascaded through me. Why was I surprised? It wasn't like I had expectations that they gave a crap about me.

Jack leaned forward and reached into his back pocket. He pulled what looked like a Polaroid and set it on the table.

"Is that you?" Chav asked me. "Cripes, you were young."

My hair was dark and pulled back into a ponytail. I was smiling, my face bright with what I thought was love. "I was seventeen," I said. My boyfriend, the boy I'd lost my virginity to, had taken the picture a week before my eighteenth birthday. The week before I left. He was supposed to run away with me, but he'd chickened out.

"What does it say on the white part?" Willy asked. "It's pretty faded."

I moved out of Babe's arms, staring at the young girl in the picture. I didn't even recognize her anymore. "You ruined my life. I never want to speak to you again. I hate you," I said, reciting the words on the photo from memory. "How did Jerry and Rhonda end up with this photo?"

"They said you left it for them," Jack answered.

I frowned. "I didn't leave it for them." I'd left it for the jerk who broke my heart. I had no idea how my parents ended up with it.

"Who'd you leave it for then?" Jack asked.

"Moonbell Lowenstein," I told him.

"The Moonbell?" Chav asked.

"Same." I'd told her everything about my life, including all the poor choices I'd made when it came to guys.

Willy guffawed. "What a dumb name."

"It really is," I agreed. "But that's a story for a *never* time."

"Okay," Jack said. "Well, I found this a month ago." He tapped the photograph. "At first, I thought it was a picture of Mom from when she was young."

"What did she say when you asked about it?"

"She cried," he said. "Then she told me you'd run away as a teenager. She was really upset."

"But not upset enough to try and find me." Not that I'd wanted them to. My life had been just fine without them. Better, actually.

"She said they'd hired a private detective after you took off. He found you in San Diego. They sent letters. Even tried to call. They figured they'd ruined their chance to be in your life." Jack looked at me, sincerity in his gaze. "They backed off. Figured that was what you wanted."

Until this moment, I thought never speaking or seeing my parents again was what I wanted. But now? Doubt swirled through me. "That must have been after I finally received my delayed birth certificate and social security number. I would have been untraceable until then." I'd had to jump through some major hoops and save up money for forged school documents and such before the state would issue me a birth certificate. I didn't know how to feel about my parents hiring a detective to find me. On one hand, it was a total violation of privacy. On the other hand, they'd cared enough to track me down. "They hired a private eye, huh? I'm surprised they didn't try tracking me down with a divining stone and a celestial map."

Jack blinked. "I can't imagine they'd ever do something like that. They're too... grounded in reality."

I held up my hand. "Grounded in reality? Are we talking about the same parents who hung crystals all over my room and anointed my bed with patchouli and sage smudge weekly because they believed it would make my psychic ability grow stronger while I slept?"

"The crystals sound pretty," Ruth said.

I sat down then forced myself to smile. "It was a long time ago." And just one of my many unsettling memories. I always felt like a commodity to them. "They used me to make themselves more important to the leaders of the commune."

Ruth thrust some pumpkin pie in front of me. "Here. Eat this. You'll feel better."

I wasn't sure pie could fix how I was feeling, but I was willing to give it a shot. "Thanks." I took a bite. The firm, but creamy texture, made the sweet, spiced pumpkin perfect, and the whipped cream cut the richness in a way that made me want to eat the whole pie by myself. "Okay, this does make me feel better."

Willy's phone beeped. She looked at the screen. "It's Brady. He said that they made it to the park with the kids."

"Were we worried they wouldn't make it?" Chavvah asked.

I snorted whip cream out my nose then proceeded to inhale a chunk of crust into my windpipe. I staggered up from the chair, coughing, gagging, and sneezing. I knocked a cup of water onto the ground, and when I tried to step around it, I slipped and landed on my elbow and hip.

Babe, Chav, Ruth, Willy, and Jack were instantly up and kneeling next to me and trying to help me up. The crust had dislodged, and while I was still wheezy, I could breathe again. "I am such a clutz," I rasped. The situation reminded me of Baby Jude's birth.

Jack touched my wrist. "Are you okay?"

I locked eyes with him, and...

Jeremiah Bowers, the owner of the Paw-On pawn shop, waved a gun at me.

A pain deep in my abdomen sent me careening forward. "Something's wrong," I said.

"Hello," Jeremiah said. He thrust the gun toward me and Babe's Aunt Erma Jean. "I have a gun!"

"And I'm having pain," I yelled. It felt as if I'd been kicked in the stomach by a mule.

"You're having a baby," Erma Jeans said.

"Don't you think I know that?" I asked her. "I'm five months pregnant for heaven's sake."

"I mean now." She gestured to the ground.

My thighs were wet, my shoes soaked, and a big puddle of clear fluid was spreading across the smooth concrete floor. "Oh, jeezus."

"I don't care if you're giving birth to the Messiah himself, get your butt over here," Jeremiah ordered.

I tried to comply with his demands, but I slipped on the amniotic fluid and fell backward. I grabbed a nearby shelf to stop my fall. It gave without warning. A large bottle of red dye number four shattered on the concrete. Its crimson liquid splashed my dress. Erma Jean attacked Jeremiah. Another contraction hit me. Where was Babe? I needed Babe.

"Sunny?" a man said. I turned and saw a young man with golden brown hair. His eyes were kind, slightly turned down at the corners. They reminded me of my dad's eyes.

"Get help," I told him, groaning as the pain increased.

"Let it go," he said.

I cried out as the pressure grew unbearable.

My eye's widened when Erma Jean roared as she partially transformed into a werecoyote and ripped Jeremiah apart. After, she ran to my side.

The man shook his head, his eyes wide with fear. "Let go of my hand."

I looked. My hand was outstretched, holding his, and I couldn't for the life of me remember why. I let go as if I were holding a live wire, and...

"Sunny!" Babe said, pulling me up into his arms. "Are you okay?"

"I'm fine," I told him. I glanced at my brother and stared at him. The memory had been real. Or at least, it had felt real down to every detail. Except for him. He'd been there. I looked at Chav. I knew what she'd meant now.

"How did you do that?" I asked him.

"I can travel into the past whenever I touch someone, but only if they are thinking about something very specific. It has to be a memory with a strong emotional bond with the person, otherwise it doesn't work."

"When I'd slipped it made me think of the birth of my son."

"And then you took us there," Jack said. He was pale now. And sweating.

"Are you sick?"

"His heart rate is increased," Willy said.

"He smells like fear," Babe said. "You better sit down, Jack."

"That woman." Jack sat down and shook his head. "She turned into a monster when she killed that man. She turned into a giant hairy monster."

I flushed guiltily. So much for keeping the human in the dark about therianthropes.

I looked at Jack, and as calmly as I could, I said, "That was no monster. That was Great Aunt Erma Jean."

CHAPTER 4

Babe took me aside into the living room while my besties worked to soothe Jack's anxiety with maple butter sweet potato mash and hickory smoked ham.

"This is not good," Babe said. "Humans can't know about us."

"Then I guess we take him out to the woods and whack him. You get the wheelbarrow, and I'll get a shovel."

"Don't be ridiculous, Sunny," he said seriously. "I don't need a wheelbarrow. I can easily carry his body weight."

"Babe!" I smacked his chest. "I'm kidding."

He cracked a smile. "So am I." He rubbed my upper arms, gripped my shoulders, then shrugged. "I don't think it will be necessary to dispose of your brother."

"Alleged brother." I narrowed my gaze at him. "What do you mean by you don't 'think it will be necessary to dispose of' my brother?"

Babe let me go. "We should get back in there with

them." And without answering my question, he walked around me to the kitchen. I supposed that was an answer in itself.

Jack was sitting at the table still, and his face was strangely calm as he looked up at me.

"Did you all drug him?" I asked.

Willy rolled her eyes at me. "No. No drugging."

Jack cast her a wary glance then looked at the cup of warm tea sitting in front of him.

"It's not drugged," Chav said. "Honest."

I took the cup from in front of Jack and put it to my lips. No one tried to stop me. I took a sip. "Mmm. Ginger and spice with a little honey. Very calming." I also tasted kava, which had some anxiety relieving properties, but I kept that to myself. I set the cup down and pushed it over to Jack. "You can drink it."

He made a face. "You just drank from the cup."

I pressed my fingers to my chest. "Do you think I have girl cooties?"

"Around here, it won't be the germs that kill you," Willy mumbled.

"Stop it," Ruth said. "You all are making Jack nervous." She replaced the tea in front of him. "Here you go. Cootie free."

"Thank you," he said. He took a small sip then a bigger one. "This is nice."

"Enjoy," Ruth said. She raised her brows at me. "Why don't you sit down, Sunny? I'm sure it's been a big day for you, too. You and Jack should talk."

Ruth, who is the best organizer I know, shooed everyone from the kitchen but Jack and me. Before she left, she said, "Tell him whatever you feel comfortable telling him. We trust your judgment."

"Thanks." I watched as Jack stuck his finger into is tea and gave it a swirl. "Rhonda used to do that with her drinks."

"She still does." His eyes lit up. "I guess some things stay the same."

"Look, I'm really glad you had parents that were there for you. But why don't we skip the family reunion and get down to why you're here. You said you were here to warn me."

"Warn might have been a strong word."

"So, you misled me."

The corner of his eyes crinkled. "In my defense, it got me in the door."

"Okay. You're in. Now what?"

"You look a lot like her," Jack said. "I see Mom in the shape of your mouth. The curve of your jaw."

I met his gaze. "Uh huh."

"The condescending stare," he added.

I laughed. "She did have a wicked stare."

"Still does." He smiled. "You laugh like her, too."

"Are they really living in an actual house in Arkansas?"

"Yes." He pulled out his phone and tapped on the gallery. "There's my dog Juke Box, he's a boxer, in the front yard."

"He's a cutie." The white boxer was on his back in the grass. The house was a gray split-level ranch. And as a kicker, there was a mini-SUV in the driveway. "Do you have any pictures of them?"

Jack flipped past several pictures of Juke Box, a selfie, and a picture of a lake with hills in the background before landing on one of woman laughing as a man dolloped her nose with chocolate cake frosting.

I felt my skin tighten as I went slightly numb. The woman's face was definitely Rhonda, older, of course, her brunette hair now trimmed with slivers of silver and gray, and the man, he was thicker than Jerry. His once long hair was gone, replaced by short-shorn locks and a hairline that receded to the top of his head. He wore glasses, but I could see him beneath this changed exterior, and neither my brain nor my body knew how to react.

"I have a better one," Jack said.

"No," I told him. "This one's good." I shook my head, trying to shake loose the fog of past grief. "Rhonda used to have dreadlocks. And Jerry, his hair had been thick and down his back. I can't believe how--" I stood up and paced a little. "I'm sorry. This is not your drama." I stared at Jack, sitting there looking so average and boring, and I was envious of his life. He'd had two stable parents who loved him and protected him, and I had two parents who so busy trying to find themselves they never had time for me. "I think you need to tell me why you're here, Jack."

"How about if you answer a question for me, I'll answer a question for you?"

I glared at him. "How about you answer my question, and I won't have my husband take you outside for a good thrashing?"

He blanched a little but didn't give in. "My question first."

"Fine." I sighed. "What's your question?"

"Did that woman in the memory quest really turn into a half-beast?"

"Oh." I blinked. A lot. "Uhm. That's really not something humans are supposed to know about."

"You're human."

"I'm also a psychic," I said in my defense.

"Well, good news," he said. "So am I."

"Smart ass."

"I'm thinking it might run in the family," he said.

There was a fire in Jack's personality that I would normally like in someone who wasn't my long-lost sibling who had the home life I'd always dreamed about but would never have.

Jack took another sip of his tea. "Besides, most people where I'm from think I'm crazy. Who would believe me?"

I guess one of the benefits of growing up in a commune was that those drug addled minds would believe just about anything. "Where I grew up, crazy was the new normal." Most of the numbness was gone now, and the anger I had wasn't for Jack. "This is a therianthropic community," I told him. "Therianthropes are people who are also part animal."

"Like a werewolf?"

I nodded. "Yes, but different species. Werewolves are lycanthropes. We have a handful of them here in Peculiar, but most the town are therians."

"Is your husband a...therian?"

"Yep. My two kids, too." I smiled thinking about Baby Jude and Dawn running around like sweet little pups. "They are coyote shifters."

"Wow." He rubbed his hands over his face then through his hair. "Wow."

"Freaky, right?"

"How is that even possible?"

I shrugged. "You were there when Great Aunt Erma Jean went all furry terminator on Jeremiah Bowers."

"I didn't believe my eyes. I thought because you were a psychic, maybe our powers combined to create a crazy nightmare." He took another sip of tea. "I can't believe it's real."

"I'm sure you get the same reaction when you tell people you are a psychic."

He nodded. "That's true. I just never imagined there were real shapeshifters. I mean, walking through someone's memory isn't the same thing as physically changing body form."

"How does your ability work?"

"If someone is thinking of a specific time in their lives, and they focus on the moment and how it made them feel, I can connect with that, and take us both back to the time and place. Memory has a way of fading and changing. My ability allows my clients to see things as they really happened. I use it to settle disputes, find lost objects, and relive happier times. I take them back to the desired moment and they get to relive it all over again."

"So, it's more like time travel than a vision."

"Sort of, but I can only observe, not interact," he explained. "I'm the fly on the wall."

"But Chavvah said you were at her wedding, like she remembered you being there. And I saw you at the Paw-On when I went into labor. You were holding my hand."

"Yeah," he agreed. "That really freaked me out. I've never had anyone talk to me in a vision, and even stranger, I couldn't stop the memory walk. You were keeping me there. It was only after you let go that I could take us out of it. And I hadn't realized that your friend saw me, either, though it didn't feel nearly as intense as when I was in the memory with you." He scratched his chin. "I would love to try it with someone else to make sure it's not a fluke."

I snorted. "You want to experiment on my family and friends? I don't think so."

Chav popped her head around the corner. "It could be interesting," she said.

Of course, they were listening. "Who in their right mind wants a stranger poking around in their past?"

"Honestly, I really enjoyed reliving my wedding," she said. "It was a good day, you know, other than my step-daughter trying to kill me and all."

"I'll do it," Babe said as he walked into the kitchen.

Ruth followed him in. "I'd volunteer, as well."

Willy, who look particularly grumpy, said, "This is a fucking terrible idea."

I crossed my arms. "I take it you have no plans to sign up to relive the past."

She smirked. "I'd rather shit the bed."

"That's pretty definitive," Chav said. "Willy's out."

"I'm excited to try this. Who's up first?" Jack asked.

I waved my hand at him. "Wait a minute there, Jack-o. Slow your jelly roll."

He pinched his thin, flat belly. "I have no jelly roll."

Another strike against him. "I have enough jelly roll to slow for the two of us."

"Why aren't you more scared of us?" Willy asked. "A smart man would be looking for escape routes."

"I kind of figure if you all were going to hurt me, you'd have done it by now," Jack answered. "I'm chancing that you're willing to let me keep breathing, at least for now. Besides, where would I go? My car is sitting at the police station miles from here, and I don't see me getting far on foot if you guys want to catch me."

Willy pursed her lips and gave him a grudging nod. "All true."

"I promise to stop any memory that is unpleasant or too personal."

"Don't think about sex anyone," I said then giggled. That's all they'd be thinking about now.

Ruth and Babe were quiet for a moment, then Ruth said, "Babe better go first."

Chav and Willy both snickered until Ruth cast her glare on them.

Babe raised his hand. "Fine. I'll do it." He gave me a baleful glance. "But, remember, if your brother sees you naked, it's your fault, not mine."

CHAPTER 5

"**A**ll right," Jack said. He and Babe were sitting across from each other now. "I want you to think of a pleasant memory, one that you feel a strong connection with."

"But not one that involves me getting naked," I added.

"To be on the safe side," Jack said, "why don't you pick a time from before you met Sunny?"

A flash of my husband with the evil dead, aka Sheila Murphy, the woman who used to boff him and who tried to kill me, made me cringe. "Pick a time before you came to Peculiar," I told Babe. I gave him a tight smile with lots of teeth.

He winked at me. "I've chosen my moment."

"When you're ready, I'm going to touch your hand. Just relax into the memory," Jack said.

Babe shook his hands and arms, cracked his neck and took a couple of deep breaths. "Ready."

"For a rumble," Willy said.

Ruth giggled.

Babe curled his lip. "Let's just get this over with."

"Are you having second thoughts?" I asked.

Hesitantly, he said, "No. Maybe some third or fourth thoughts, but no second ones."

Chav gave him a nudge. "It doesn't hurt, baby bro. You know, in case you were worried." She held up her hands. "See. No bruises."

Babe slid his hand, palm up across the table to Jack. "Do it."

Jack, like with Chav, stretched out a finger and made just the slightest contact with Babe's skin. He jerked again, his eyes rolling back. It reminded me of the pre-vision seizures I had sometimes.

"Is it working?" Willy asked.

Ruth hushed her. "Give them a minute."

Babe's blue eyes closed. His lids began to flutter.

"He's in it now," Chav said.

His face was serene, the muscles relaxed. "I wonder where he chose to go?" I asked.

Chav tilted her head as she studied her brother. "He's probably reliving some touchdown he scored on the football field in high school. Mom and Dad used to brag about his games all the time."

Chav was six years older than Babe, so she wasn't around when he was in high school, but I imagined he was a great athlete, and not just because he was a shifter. My dude had some serious hand-eye coordination that I'm sure translated to sports. He and Chav had grown up as integrators, therians who lived among humans. The freedom the shifters had in Peculiar didn't translate to the real world.

I asked him once if it was hard to constantly hide who he was, and he said, "I hid my nature, not who I am. There's a difference."

I never really understood, though. I spent a lifetime hiding who and what I was from everyone. Except Chav. Even now, I had a core group of friends in Peculiar who knew I was human and not a shifter, but I still had to hide a part of myself from everyone else around here. The Tri-state council, the head shifter mucky-mucks, wouldn't take kindly to a human living in a therian town. We'd already survived one investigation, but it had been tough. If I'd been found out, Babe and I would have been forced to leave town, and he would have had to return to inte-gration. I wondered if Babe would have been happier to return to the human world. He had a degree in public relations, and before his brother and sister's disappear-ances brought him to Peculiar, he had lined up a job in Kansas City.

Since I never wanted to leave Peculiar, I didn't ask him. Did I think I was being a coward? Absolutely. But I'd learned a long time ago not to ask questions when I wasn't sure I'd like the answer.

"Is he crying?" Ruth asked.

A tear fell down Babe's cheek. What in the world could he be experiencing that would upset him enough to cry? And why wasn't Jack bringing them back?

"Jack, stop this." Alarm and a fierce protectiveness rushed through me. "Babe. Wake up."

Neither of them moved. My heart picked up the pace. Instinctually, I grabbed Babe's hand to break the contact, but when my fingers connected, my skin warmed as my country-style kitchen disappeared and was replaced with an Old World style kitchen with dark, carved wood cabinets that went all the way to the ceiling, a granite-topped center island, and bisque-colored tiles. A bounty of food including turkey, stuffing, gelatin salads, mashed potatoes, gravy, yams with marshmallows, and all the other traditional Thanksgiving fixings covered every ounce of counter space.

My mother-in-law Celia was stirring a crockpot of green beans and a young boy, about the age of ten sat at the end of a breakfast bar eating celery packed with peanut butter. He smiled at his mom, his blue eyes sparkling. He hopped down and quietly made his way to the turkey, but before he could even lay one finger on the bird, Celia whipped around and said, "Don't you dare, young man." Her own smile took the harshness out of her words. "Why don't you take the salads to the dining room table?" Then she looked up, and yelled, "Jude! Chav! Come help your brother set the table. It's that time!"

"My gosh. That's Babe," I said.

Jack said, "It is."

"Can he see you?"

"No. I haven't been able to interact with him. Not like with you and Chavvah. This is nice, though."

"Did something bad happen? He's upset."

Jack chuckled. "He isn't upset. He's happy."

A brown-haired teenaged boy, who I realized was his older brother Jude, rushed into the room. He was tall but hadn't quite grown into his lank yet. He put Babe in a headlock and rubbed Babe's scalp with his knuckles.

"Mom!" Babe said.

"You boys quit roughhousing," Celia told. "Get the food moving in the right direction before I sick Aunt Erma Jean on you."

They both made shows of dramatic dismay. Celia laughed.

"You two need to quit being so annoying," a young Chavvah said as she trailed into the kitchen.

Jude released Babe, and both boys gave each other a knowing look, before shouting, "Tickle torture!" and tackling their sister to ground.

They were laughing and loving and being a family, and I suddenly understood why Babe had gotten emotional.

"I'm tired," Jack said. "Time passes quickly in these memory quests, and I don't think I can sustain this one much longer."

"He really does look happy," I said, watching my husband relive what had to be a favorite childhood memory. "They all do." The Trimmels had suffered such a great loss when Jude died. I didn't realize just how big until now.

"You have to let go, Sunny. I think your contact is keeping us here. The same thing happened in your memory. I couldn't bring us out of it. You have to be the one."

"Okay." The Old World kitchen disappeared, and I was once again sitting at the table in my own cozy space.

Babe looked dazed. "That was...unsettling."

"What happened?" Chav asked.

"Yeah, spill," Willy added.

Ruth didn't say anything, but she looked eager.

"I was thinking about Thanksgiving when I was a kid, and *bam*, I was there," Babe said.

"Was Aunt Erma Jean complaining about the noise? Was Dad passed out on the couch? He never lasted more than a few minutes once the meal was over."

Babe forced a slight smile. "I didn't get that far."

"Jude was there," I said. "And you, Chav. You guys were having a tickle fight."

"Tickle torture." She grimaced. Her eyes grew melancholy. "Jude and Babe used to get me all the time. Which Thanksgiving?" she asked her brother.

"The last one before you moved to California. The last one we were all together."

"Oh." She smiled sadly. "That was a good Thanksgiving."

"The best," he agreed.

I patted my husband's hand. "Your mom really knew how to cook for an army."

He was quiet for a moment then said, "Wait. How do you know? And how did you know about the tickle fight?"

"When I touched you to try and break the memory link with Jack, I was somehow pulled in. Did you see either Jack or me when you were in the kitchen with your mom?"

"I didn't. It was all very clear. Really like I was there, that it was happening right then and not twenty years ago." Babe laced his fingers with mine. "It was nice seeing my brother again. Experiencing my family before we'd lost each other."

"I could see Jack when we visited my wedding. What's the difference between Babe and me?"

"I have a theory," I told them. "Remember when we connected psychically because of Brother Wolf when those psychos were stalking you?"

"You guys have colorful lives around here," Jack said.

"You don't even know," Willy agreed.

Chavvah nodded. "I remember. Brother Wolf showed you and me, through your vision, my past and my present."

My throat felt thick as I thought about her spirit guide showing me Chav, beaten and broken, lying on the ground. She'd been tortured all for the pleasure of hunters. I shook the image from my mind. "He allowed you to see my vision, to share it with me. Maybe when that door opened, it stayed open."

"And maybe because you and Jack share the same psychic bloodline, you got to share his vision!" Ruth said enthusiastically.

I pointed at her. "Give that girl a cookie."

Ruth rubbed her hands together. "You know I love a good cookie."

"A fortune cookie," Willy said. "Get it, because you guys are psychic. Fortune telling."

"We get it, girl." I shook my head. "It's just not that funny."

"Yes, it was," she said on a giggle.

I smirked. "The teensiest bit."

"Okay, Jack. We've done your experiment. Now, it's time for you to answer my question. What are you doing here? Why come find me?"

Ruth's phone vibrated on the counter. She checked it. "Ed wants to know if we are still having dinner here today. If not, he'll take the kids to the Blonde Bear."

"We are eating here," I snapped. I pointed at all the food in crockpots. "Crap, the stuffing is in the fridge still. It needs to go in the oven."

"Do you want the guys to bring the children back?" Ruth gestured to my brother. "I mean, you already told Jack about us."

"Fine." I sighed then glared at Jack. "Don't freak out if our kids go furry and run around on four legs."

"Is that something that happens a lot?"

"Yep."

Chav opened the fridge and pulled out a foil-covered pan. "I'll get the stuffing going. Willy can take care of the mashed potatoes, and Ruth will do the gravy."

"We need to get the turkey out of the cooler and get it heated up, too," I said.

"We'll handle it," Chav told me. "You and Jack have a lot to talk about. So, you go do that, and we'll do this." She turned the oven on to get it preheated. "Go. Talk to your brother."

CHAPTER 6

I took Jack out back for privacy. Plus, Baby Jude was nearly four now and was going through a "why?" phase. I didn't want to introduce him to his supposed uncle until I knew I could trust Jack. Wait. What? Was I actually beginning to accept I had a brother?

"Please tell me you have dragons," Jack said. He was staring at the fire blackened grass.

"They do make great pets," I said.

His eyes bulged. "You've got to be kidding."

"Of course, I'm kidding." I rolled my eyes. "There's no such things as dragons."

"Until about half an hour ago, I didn't think there was any such things as shifters and werewolves."

"Fair point." I gestured toward some bench seating Babe and I had set up under a large silver maple. Unfortunately, this late in the year, the leaves that were left on the tree had already gone from vibrant orange to a dead brown. Babe had spent the day before raking up scads of the fallen leaves. "Let's sit over there."

Jack was wearing his jacket, but he gave his arms a quick rub then put on his gloves after we sat down.

It was fifty degrees out, but I felt comfortable enough in my sweater. Since December, I had been changed. A wedding gift for Chav from Brother Wolf. He'd told her that he wanted to make her happy, and he knew that having me in her life was a good start. He didn't turn me into a therianthrope. That was a gene you had to be born with. However, he granted me the long life of one, which meant that my body adapted to cold and heat better than an average human, I was more resistant to colds and flus, and my aging process had slowed way down. Thank heavens. I was already a decade older than my husband, and I had worried more than once about what our lives would be like forty years from now. His second gift to her was the gorgeously cheerful Rory. Though, if he'd only been doling out one gift that day, I would have gladly given up a long life so that she could have her baby.

I pivoted on the bench to face Jack. "This is the last time I'm going to ask. Why are you here? You said you had a warning, so give it to me."

"Mom was diagnosed with cancer."

"I'm sorry," I said. I had to admit, if only to myself, that a part of me hurt hearing the news. "How bad is it?"

"She has something called multiple myeloma in her right thigh bone," Jack said. "She's been fighting it with chemo, steroids, and blood transfusions for almost a year now."

"Is it working?"

"The cancer has started to spread into her hip."

"Is there any way to stop it?"

"The doctors are looking for a bone marrow match. Unfortunately, I was only a thirty-eight percent match, and they need at least fifty percent for a transplant." He sighed. "If they can't find one, they will have to amputate. Even then, there is no guarantees they can get all the cells."

I frowned, more sad than angry. Rhonda had found a way to try and use me again. "Is that why you came here, Jack? Rhonda wants my bone marrow, so she sent you to guilt me into it?"

"I told you, she doesn't know I'm here. When I brought up trying to find you, she said no."

I don't know which was worse, feeling used or feeling as if I didn't matter. "She is still the selfish Rhonda I remember."

"You know how I found your picture?" He shoved his gloved hands into his pockets. "She was in so much pain that I was searching for her pain pills in her bedside stand. Your picture was in there. She never forgot you. I think she doesn't want to reach out because she's...."

"Stubborn, prideful, a terrible mom," I supplied.

"Ashamed," Jack said. "I think she's really ashamed. When I asked her about you, I'd never seen her look so miserable, and she's on some really strong chemo, so that's saying a lot." He took his hands out of his pockets and took off the glove on his right hand. "Look, you strike me as the kind of person who would go to great lengths to help someone in their time of need. If it helps, think of Mom as a stranger."

"I don't have to think of her as a stranger. She is a stranger. I don't know this person you keep talking about. She isn't the same Rhonda who let me raise myself because she couldn't be bothered."

Jack's eyes crested with tears. "Can I show you my mother? I know you hate her, but I love her. I don't want her to lose her leg." He took a steadying breath. "Or worse. Die."

"Fine. But just because I'm looking doesn't mean I'm saying yes to anything."

"Agreed," Jack said. He held out his hand.

I took it.

"Jack!" a woman yelled. "Can you come down and help me?"

Jack and I were sitting on the edge of a full-sized bed in a clean bedroom. There were inspirational quotes on the walls, like "Be the best you and you will always be the best."

Jack looked at me. "Mom loves inspirational quotes."

"She was always spouting that kind of crap when I was growing up." I rolled my eyes. " What year is this?"

"This is thanksgiving last year, before her cancer diagnosis." He stood up. "Come on."

When we exited his bedroom, I could smell the combined scents of turkey and fresh baked apple pie. "The desserts smell good," I said.

"Mom can't bake to save her life." Jack laughed. "But she knows how to buy really great scented candles."

"That's the Rhonda I remember," I said, smiling despite myself. I felt nervous, and vision me was experiencing sweaty palms. "Is this normal?"

He chuckled. "There's not a damn thing normal about any of this. I'm making it up as I go along. I've never walked my own memory quest. Until a few seconds ago, I wasn't sure it was possible."

"That's so reassuring."

We passed the open door of a hallway bathroom and two closed doors before we walked through a family room with two recliners, a couch, end tables, a coffee table, and a large screen television over a fireplace mantle. Near the mantle was a built-in bookshelf. with framed pictures placed across one shelf. "Can I go look?"

"I don't know," he said. "I went right to the kitchen when she called, but I'm not sure what rules we're following now."

I let go of his hand to make my way across the room.
*****

"Well, now we know that I can't break from the memory," I told Jack as we sat next to each other on the bench in my back yard. "Let's try again. This time, I won't veer from the memory."

He took my hand again.
*****

We passed through the living room under an arch into the kitchen. Rhonda, her hair cut shoulder length with natural waves, looking very much like the picture I'd seen on Jack's phone, lit up when her son walked into the room.

"Come here and help me," she said.

"Sure, Mom. What do you need?"

"Can you get the cakes out of the freezer so they can thaw?"

"Cake for Thanksgiving?" I asked.

"Don't judge," Jack said to me. His mother didn't seem to notice. Which meant, he could talk outside the memory, but it didn't have an effect on how things played out. "Pepperidge Farm Fudge cake is really good, and Mom stacks it so it's nice and tall."

"But for Thanksgiving?"

"Mom's not a great cook," he said, pulling the boxed cakes from the freezer side of the refrigerator. He put them on the counter. It was weird, because I could still feel myself holding his hand, but I could also see him acting through the memory.

"You want me to take them out of the boxes?" he asked.

"That would be nice." She leaned over and kissed his offered cheek. "You're a good kid."

He grimaced. "Where's Dad?"

"You know your father," she said. "He's at the rescue mission, serving Thanksgiving dinner." She looked at a clock on the wall. "He said he'd be done by four and it's a little after now, so he should be home any minute."

She stirred some kind of sludge in a pot. It smelled like feet.

"What is that?" I hissed.

"Oyster dressing," he said. "It's gross, but tradition."

I shuddered as Rhonda used a tasting spoon to take a bite. "Some traditions should be retired."

Rhonda began to hum. I blanched, feeling sicker than when she ate the oyster stuffing, when I realized it was "You Are My Sunshine," a song she used to sing when she would put me to bed.

"I can't," I said. I tried to let go of Jack's hand, but he held on.

"Wait, Sunny. Dad will be home soon. In a few minutes, he will walk in the door. Just wait."

"This hurts too much. Don't you understand that Jack? No." I shook my head. "How could you? You've had this ideal childhood with all its bad oyster stuffing and chocolate cake holidays. You don't know the kind of pain they put me through. This isn't the Thanksgiving I remember, and I am sorry, but I can't watch them give you what they could never give me."

"Show me," he said. He took both my hands. "Show me how bad it was. Make me understand."

*****

The pungent scent of patchouli incense and the slightly skunky aroma of pot filled the space around me. I felt strange and slightly panicked as I looked around. There was a nylon screen around my afghan covered bedroll. Crystals hung down on fishing line, causing a twinkling of lights that mimicked the stars on my makeshift walls.

"Ruth was right. It really is pretty," Jack said. "When are we?"

I looked at him, fighting down the panic and anxiety churning in my gut. "How old do I look to you?"

"Fourteen or fifteen," he said.

I groaned.

"What?" he asked. "What is it?"

"This is the harvest festival when I had my first psychic vision."

CHAPTER 7

"This is a yurt!" Jack exclaimed.

"Yep," I said sourly. "It sure is."

"How freaking cool! You really lived in a yurt."

"So cool," I told him. "I just loved the lack of privacy, especially being able to hear Rhonda and Jerry having sex just a couple of thin flaps away was a highlight of my childhood."

"That's revolting," Jack said.

"Welcome to yurt living, my friend." Yurts are round tents, and ours had been sectioned off for two semi-private sleeping areas and one communal space with three bean bags and handwoven rugs. Incense was burning in a small brass holder. "Take a good look. It's a nice place to visit, but you wouldn't want to live here." At least, I never had.

"I don't know," Jack said. "It's interesting."

"Says a guy who never had to hear his mom moan his dad's name."

"Again," Jack said. "Revolting."

"Come on. My fourteen-year-old self wants to get on the on the move."

"It's a strange sensation, right? My vision self, kept wanting to move with the memory, even when I was talking to you." Jack walked with me out the front flap into the wild and whacky. "That man's not wearing pants," he said in a harsh whisper.

A guy with greasy tangled hair, a poncho and no pants, was pouring himself a cup of coffee from a camp-fire kettle outside a small tent. His ill-fitting boots were covered with mud. "That's Pervy Pete," I said. "He takes free-balling to new levels. He's relatively harmless. I just keep a healthy distance."

Jack stumbled a little as we gave Pete a wide berth. "When did your vision happen?"

"Soon, I think. I remember I'd gotten mad at Rhonda for making me take part in the harvest festival medita-tion circle in the morning. They thought positive thoughts could bring the rain, but it had been raining all week, and I was pretty much over the wet and the mud.

My feet sloshed in sopping earth as we walked, but I noticed Jack's were nice and dry. He grinned. "Not my memory. Since I'm not really here, I'm not affected."

"Lucky," I told him. "I'm cold and miserable."

"Where are we going?"

"There's a basket weaving group just up ahead." I pointed to a large rectangular shelter over a concrete pad. A dozen kids ranging from five to eighteen sat at picnic tables. A young man with blond hair and the bluest eyes waved at me. I smiled and waved back. I didn't want to, but the memory made me.

"Who is that?"

"Moonbell," I told him. "The boy who will, in a few years, crush young Sunny Haddock's heart."

"Where are Mom and Dad?"

"I can't remember," I said. At the time, I only had eyes for Moonbell. Even if Rhonda and Jerry had been around, I'm not sure I would have noticed.

I sat down in the spot Moonbell had saved for me. "Hey, Sunshine," he said. "I saved some husks for you."

I wanted to tell him where he could shove his husks, but instead, I giggled. "You are so thoughtful, Moonbell." Adult me was gagging hard.

Jack had a grin on his face that made me want to punch him. "Stop it," I told him. "I was fifteen-years-old."

"Moonbell seems like quite a catch," he teased.

"I thought so at the time."

Speaking of Moonbell, he pushed his shoulder against mine. "You coming to the swinging bridge tonight?"

"I don't know if I can. Rhonda wants me to go with her to the women's menstrual party."

"Bummer," Moonbell said.

"You meant minstrel? Like singers, lutes, mandolins," Jack said, his expression horrified.

"Nope. You heard me right the first time. The women around here loved to celebrate their flow, if you catch my meaning."

Jack winced. "I've not only caught, I've taken it off the hook, and I'm throwing it back."

I laughed. "Good one."

"Maybe you can sneak away," Moonbell said. "Once all that sweat and smoke gets going, no one will notice if you crawl out of the tent." He put his hand on my knee and smiled, his dimples deepening into a cuteness my fifteen-year-old self couldn't resist.

"Okay," I said. "I'll sneak out after the miracle of life lecture."

"Great," he said. "It's a date."

My stomach squeezed and my heart fluttered. "It's a date." Ugh. I hated myself. I wished I could go back and tell young Sunny to kick Moonbell in his miracle of life.

"Are you okay?" Jack asked.

I was still smiling when I met his gaze. "Don't I look all right?"

"It feels like you are going to break my fingers," he said.

"Oh." I loosened my grip. "There's just so many bad memories."

"I don't see how. Everyone looks so peaceful and happy here."

"Because everyone's on drugs," I told him.

"What happens next?"

"Can we fast forward?" I was not in the mood to basket weave with Moonbell anymore.

"Sunny!" A girl with ratty strawberry blonde curls and a smattering of freckles across her pert nose skipped up to our table.

"Hey, Tabs," I said with mild irritation. I remembered being annoyed that she was interrupting my time with the boy I liked, but my adult self thought of Tabitha

Holloway fondly. She'd been my best friend since we were five. "Do you need something?" I asked her.

The corners of her eyes crinkled, and her lips pursed. I'd hurt her feelings. "Did you want to go get hot cocoa? Jacoby just made some fresh."

Jacoby was her father. I rolled my eyes at her then glanced at Moonbell for approval. "Only babies drink hot cocoa," I said.

"Oh. Okay." Her lower lip trembled slightly. "Maybe next time."

"I don't remember this happening," I told Jack. "I kind of remember her asking me about the hot chocolate, but I don't recall being this awful to her." In my current life, I couldn't imagine being that way with Chav, or really any of my friends.

"What is it they say about history being written by the winners? I think memory is a lot like that as well. We tend to forget or misremember when we do things that stray from what we consider our own moral code. Our brain rewrites those moments and sometimes does away with them completely."

What he meant was, people tended to revise the moments in their life where they might have been the bad guy. Tabs and I had grown apart during my teenage years, and from that small interaction, I was certain it was my fault.

"I wish I could tell her I was sorry," I told Jack. "She deserved a better friend."

Jack nodded. "I get it." He looked around. "This place is pretty busy. How many people live here?"

"I don't know?" My little hands were inexpertly

weaving the cornhusk into what looks like a misshapen bowl. "About a hundred or so."

"Here, Sunshine," Moonbell said, reaching an arm around me. He pulled on one of the husks. "If you pull this tighter it will curl for the sides."

I giggled.

"Shoot me now," I told Jack.

"I think it's sweet," he said. "The boy was pretty smooth."

"He was the cutest boy in the cult, and he had his pick of girls."

"But he chose you," Jack said.

"Yeah, he chose me." Until he didn't. I didn't know why I was still so mad at him. My life had turned out better than I ever dreamed. I looked at Moonbell, and his deeply dimpled cheeks. He'd made life bearable at the commune. Maybe it was time I let go of my anger. If he had come with me, I would have never found the life I was truly meant to find.

"Sunshine! Yoo hoo!" I heard a woman yell.

I clucked my tongue with disgust. "Hide me," I whined to Moonbell. "It's Rhonda."

"She's not so bad," he said.

"Yeah," I said to him. "Not so bad."

Cripes, I just said whatever I thought this guy wanted to hear. "I really don't remember being this way," I told Jack.

He chuckled. "Wow, I can't believe Mom had dreadlocks."

"I told you." And double wow, she looked so young. I always thought she looked so old when I was a teenager.

Ancient even. But she wasn't. She wore a bohemian maxi-dress cinched at the waist, showing a really flattering figure. She didn't wear any make up but didn't need to. She was beautiful.

Fifteen-year-old Sunny got up from the table, embarrassed that her mom was walking toward her and Moonbell. She did not want to talk to Rhonda in front of any of her friends. Especially not the boy she adored. "I'll see you tonight," I said quickly and quietly to Moonbell.

He nodded. "See you then."

When I reached my mom, I said, "What do you want?"

Her smile faded. "Jerry is waiting for us to have a picnic in the pasture."

"It's too muddy," I told her.

"Jerry has gone through a lot of trouble to make us a nice meal," Rhonda said. "And it would be uncharitable to flake on him."

"I think it's uncharitable to make me sit in a yucky wet field, eating stale bread and leftover soup." Oh my gosh, I'd forgotten about leftover soup. It was basically, a week's worth of leftovers thrown into a pot on Saturdays. Sometimes it was tasty, but most of the time, it had reminded me of what I thought prison food would be like.

"You're going," she said.

"Fine," I told her. "But I won't like it."

"I wouldn't expect you to," Rhonda said.

I jerked my hand from Jack's.

*****

"Are you sure you're not manipulating my memories? I remember some of this, but I don't remember Rhonda sounding like a human being. And I definitely don't remember her wanting to hang around with me unless she was showing me off."

Jack narrowed his gaze at me. "Sunny, seeing is believing. Why don't we go to the part where you had your first vision? Think back to that moment."

I gave him a skeptical look. "Will a vision in a vision make things super weird?"

"Seeing my mom with dreads has thrown me straight past weird and into bizarro-land," he said. "It's so strange seeing her so young and healthy."

I heard the pain in his words. "I'm sorry, Jack."

"Can we try again? Please. There's a reason your mind took us to that day."

I nodded. I wondered if he would like the Rhonda he saw when I took him back. She'd been so excited by my vision, that she'd turned me into a side-show commune attraction. I thought to the moments before my vision. I'd been sitting in the women's tent, and we were all sitting cross-legged and saying, "Whoosh," as we made flowing gestures with our hands from our inner thighs toward the smoky fire pit. The flames and smoke were supposed to take any bad juju our bodies had created up and out of our lives.

Jack took my hand and then we were there.

"Some of these women aren't wearing shirts!" he said. His eyes nearly popped from his head when he saw Rhonda sans top and no bra. He quickly averted his gaze and stared straight into the fire.

"Need some brain bleach?" I asked.

"Yes," he said with all seriousness. "I need a whole truckload."

I snorted. "Now you know what it's like to see your parents naked." I looked over at Rhonda and had to admit that she had nice boobs. Small and perky.

I found myself biding my time, waiting for my moment when the tent would really get cloudy, so I could escape to be with Moonbell.

"Take the hand of the person next you," Lizabet Elderberry, a gray-haired woman with wiry curls ordered. She was the oldest in the group, a leader of sorts, and I was pretty sure Elderberry wasn't her real last name. Some of my friends used to call her Lizardbutt Dingleberry.

Or maybe it was just me.

Anyways. I took Jackie Townsend's hand because she was to the right of me, and that's when it happened.

The air is cold, the railing damp. I can hear the water rushing below. The rain for the past week has picked up the current. I want to fly, soar over the mountains, and be free. Death would be the ultimate freedom. Isn't that what we always say? What comes will come, and in the end we will be free.

I laugh. I am drunk and high, and I can fly. I pull myself up, holding tight to the uprights as my feet cling precariously to the slick railing.

"I feel so alive!" I scream, hoping the words will make it true. "So alive."

"Hey!" I hear a boy shout. "Someone go and get help. He's going to jump."

"Don't do it, Pete!" I hear another boy say. It's Moonbell. They are at the bridge.

When I came to, I was outside the tent, and Rhonda was holding my hand while Lizabet patted my forehead with a damp rag.

"The smoke must have gotten to her," the gray-haired woman said.

"Pervy Pete," I muttered. "Pete."

"What about Pete?" Rhonda asked me. "Did he touch you? I swear to Mother Earth I will fucking kill him."

"I don't remember her cussing like that," I told Jack, who was on the other side of me holding my hand and craning his neck to look as far away from Rhonda's breasts as possible.

"She can be feisty," he replied. "Your vision, it was so disorientating."

"Tell me about it." I looked at Rhonda. "I saw him on the bridge. He's going to jump. I saw him. You have to save him."

"Saw him?" Lizabet asked. "Like in a vision?"

I nodded as my headache eased. "Some of the boys are at the swinging bridge. They're coming to tell you. Pete is about to fall into the river."

Just then, Lollipop Danvers came running into our camp. "He's going to jump!" he shouted. "We need help."

Rhonda looked at me. "Sunshine. You have the psychic gift," she said. "I never thought." She brushed hair away from my face. "Oh, my sweet angel."

"Maybe she is an angel," Lizabet said. "A guardian angel."

"I'm going to take her home," Rhonda said. "Can you get up?"

I nodded. Jerry ran to us. A swell of emotion filled me

when I saw him. His long hair was pulled back into a ponytail and he wore ripped up jeans and a T-shirt he'd tie-dyed himself. "Is Sunny okay?" he asked. Gosh, he looked young, too. He had kind eyes, and I remembered how calm he'd been even when Rhonda and I were at each other's throats.

Rhonda nodded. "She had a vision, Jer. An honest to goodness psychic episode." She grinned with excitement. "She's a hero, you know. She probably saved Pete's life." She slapped her thigh as they walked me back to the yurt.

I looked at Jack. "Pete saved himself," I told him while Rhonda kept rattling on about what a freaking hero I was, and how special I was. "It turned out when the boys started yelling at him not to jump, he climbed down. My ability has never been practical, and it's rarely helpful."

I took my hand from Jack's again, and we were back in my yard.

A coyote pup sprinted across the yard and leaped into my lap. I giggled as he licked my face. "Stop it, Jude."

"Jude?" Jack had moved a few inches away and was watching with curiosity. "Is this your son?"

"Yep," I told him. "And your nephew, Uncle Jack."

Jack's expression softened.

"Sorry!" Babe shouted from the back door. "I tried to stop him."

"It's fine," I said. I gave Jude a quick ear scratch and kissed his furry snout before sending him back toward the house.

"And they just run around like that all the time?" Jack asked.

"Not all the time, but yes, they do like to shift. From

what everyone tells me, the experience feels good." I smiled as Willy's toddler came running out, bursting into cougar form, while still in a diaper. "Get back here, Missy!" Willy demanded, but Missy was already climbing up a tree.

I turned to Jack. "You can see, can't you, why I don't want to see Rhonda. When I had my vision, she made it all about her. She told everyone and anyone who would listen. Heck, she had people convinced I really was a hero. They used to have me do cold readings all the time, and I'm not a very good psychic, so most of the time I would make stuff up, just to not see the disappointment on her face."

Jack shook his head. "I could be wrong, Sunny, but I saw a woman who was proud of you. It's her mother who's the psychic, Grammy Sue. Grammy told me once that Rhonda struggled being a null. Someone without ability."

"Maybe." I shook my head. "There's just too much water under that bridge, pun intended." Missy had jumped down, and now Dawn was in her little coyote form, browner than her brother, but just as cute, and she and Missy were wrestling. "Don't get into the scorched grass!" I told them. "Babe, come and make sure these kids don't get black oily soot on them. Not before dinner."

Jack smiled.

"What?" I asked.

"Moms," he said. "I think you have more in common with Rhonda than you'd like to believe."

I looked at Dawn. Would she find reason to resent me

when she was fifteen? "I don't live in a hippie dippy commune," I said.

"Neither did I," he said, "but I still went through a phase where I thought Mom and Dad were the enemy."

"But in my story, they are." I crossed my arms.

"Foods on!" Chav hollered. "Come and get it."

Missy and Dawn rolled off each other and high-tailed it to the house.

Jack and I stood up. "You go ahead," I told him. "But maybe let me borrow your phone."

He pulled it out of his jacket pocket and unlocked the screen.

He dipped his head and gave me a quick kiss on the cheek. "She's in my contacts under Mom."

When Jack headed inside, I found her number on his phone. My pulse pounded in my ears as I tapped the green call button and waited.

The woman on the other end answered. "Jack, where are you? Your grandpa said you never arrived at his house." Her voice sounded weak and strained. When I didn't respond, she said, "Is everything okay, Jack? Please talk to me."

"Rhonda," I said when I could make my voice work. My hand shook, so I pressed the phone harder to my ear. "It's me." For some reason, I couldn't say my name.

The silence on the other end lasted for only a few seconds. "Sunshine?" Her voice cracked. "I...I..."

"It's okay." My throat was thick and scratchy. "Jack is fine. He's here with me."

She was crying now. It was soft, but unmistakable.

"Thank you," she said. "It's so nice to hear your voice again. Thank you for calling me."

"Please don't cry."

"Rho?" a man asked. "Why are you crying? Are you okay? Do you need another pain pill?"

"I better go," I told her. "I didn't mean to upset you." I ended the call and sat back down on the bench as twenty years of anger and frustration culminated into uncontrollable sobbing.

Babe was there. His arm around me. He held me close and rocked me until I could breathe again.

After, he smoothed the hair from my face. My mother had done that after my vision. It was a thing that people did with the ones they loved. And she hadn't been the best mom in the world, but who was?

"What's going on?" Babe asked when a few quiet moments had passed. "Tell me, sweetheart."

"I have to go to Arkansas," I told him. "My mom needs a bone marrow transplant."

CHAPTER 8

Two weeks later...

"Are you sure you want to do this?" Rhonda asked. She was in the bed across from me at the hospital.

"I already took the five-minute shot of that stuff to make my white blood cells multiply last week, so this should be a piece of cake." It had taken less than a week for my results from the cheek swab to come back a match to my mom. I wondered if what Brother Wolf did to me would maybe give Rhonda a few more years once the transplant was completed. I hoped so.

Jerry came in the room. "You two need anything? Juice? Gelatin? I hear red is their specialty."

Rhonda smiled, but I had to admit I was freaking out a little. I'd met with my parents the weekend after Thanksgiving, and we'd all done a lot of talking, a lot of crying, apologizing, and forgiving. And in so many ways, I was glad that Jack had come into my life and brought us back together. But they hadn't been a part of my world for so long, I didn't know how to act around them. I hoped it would get easier with time.

Jack showed up with an old woman with purple-auburn hair. She had green eyes like Rhonda and me, and her smile lit up the room when she came in with him.

"Sunny," she said. "You're as beautiful in person as you are in my visions."

"You've had visions of me?"

"Of course, I have." She hobbled past Jerry to my bedside and took my hand. "I knew this day would come. I knew you would save my Rho."

"Mom," Rhonda said. "Stop that. You're going to scare Sunny off." She'd stopped calling me Sunshine, and I was glad. I wasn't that girl anymore.

"It's nice to meet you, Sue," I said to her.

"You call me Grammy Sue," she insisted.

"Okay, Grammy Sue."

She cackled and gave my hand a firm squeeze. "You're a sweet girl."

Jack glanced around the room. "Where'd Babe go?"

I said, "Down to the cafeteria for some decent coffee."

"Hah!" Jerry shook his head. "If he's waiting for decent coffee in this place, he might never return."

Jerry, Rhonda, Sue, and Jack had an easy repertoire that I envied. I'd missed so much by leaving my parents behind, but I'd also gained a lot. Maybe I'd had to lose my biological family so I could find the family of my choosing. Looking back, I wouldn't have changed a thing, because if I had, I would not have Babe and our two beautiful kiddos. And now I was in a room with my mom, dad, brother, and grandmother. So surreal.

"Hey, when this is all over, and you're well again," I told Rhonda, "Let's make plans for next Thanksgiving. Babe and I will come here." I waved my hand. "As long as you let me make the stuffing."

Jerry, without hesitation, said, "It's a deal. Can you bring the rest of the food as well?"

"Jerry!" Rhonda protested, which started a whole conversation on her lack of skill in the kitchen.

Babe snuck in amidst the debate. He kissed me so soundly my kittens sat up and purred. "You ready for all this?"

"The bone marrow donation or the new family dynamic?"

"Both," he said.

"I'm not sure I'm ready, but I am truly thankful."

The End

Note from Renee George:

HAPPY THANKSGIVING READERS,

I am so grateful to each and every one of you. I hope the holidays are filled with family, food, and festivities.

XXOO, Renee George

GONE WITH THE MINION - CHAPTER ONE

How do you save your family when they're about to lose the literal farm? You make a deal with a demon, of course. And then you spend the next one hundred and forty-nine years making him sorry he forced you to sign in blood on the dotted line.

To save her family, Southern Belle Olivia "Liv" Madder made a bargain with a demon lord and ever since, she's been haunted…by her three dead sisters, and her own guilty conscience. Every decade, since the deal, Liv has had to find a human willing to bargain their soul with Moloch. If she fails, even once, he'll not only drag her to Hell, but he'll take her sisters, too. It doesn't mean she can't make Lord Jerkface miserable in the process by removing his lesser demons from the Earthly plane.

When her latest contracted soul dies before the bargain is sealed, she has less than four days to find another soul or her own agreement will be broken. But Moloch offers her a get-out-of-Hell-free card: steal an old book once owned by paranormal researcher David Jensen. The same David Jensen she fell in love with sixty years ago but left to protect him and his family. Then Moloch drops the biggest bombshell: David has died.

Heartbroken and feeling she has no choice, Liv makes the trip to Sanctum, Missouri only to find David's grandson has the book. Worse, he's keeping a mysterious family secret that threatens Moloch, Liv, and her three sisters. What's a minion to do when her world falls apart? Get Madder than Hell and kick some demon butt.

Chapter One

It took me two seconds to spot my mark and about half that time for him to spot me. He was on the move. Right out the opened French doors. I could see he was headed toward the garden. Why, oh, why did they always run? I shoved my way through the crowd of monkey suits and silk chiffons with as much grace as I could muster.

Not an easy feat considering I was stuffed into the ill-fitting, scarlet-red, mermaid-cut, satin dress I'd…um, borrowed from the unconscious woman in the coat room. A frock more billowy and less mermaid-y would've been a better choice for running, but I'd picked this one because it matched my red stiletto pumps and my patent-leather clutch with its removable silver chain. The little purse hung off my shoulder and slapped against my thigh as I wiggled through the crowd.

I finally made it outside. Freshly blossomed lilacs burst out from the multitude of bushes like tufts of purple cotton candy and sweetened the humid air. I looked over my shoulder and saw that no one noticed, or more likely, cared that I was chasing the party's host into the lavish garden.

The three-story mansion was overly ostentatious, even for Jefferson City, the capital of Missouri. The monstrosity, with its marble columns and wrought-iron balconies, reminded me of the plantation a few miles from my father's modest farm in Georgia, where I'd been born and raised. In other words, the place stuck out like a bedazzled T-shirt at a Sunday morning church service. The owner of the mansion, Carmine Hennessy, was a lobbyist for some major companies in the northwest area of the state, and he was holding a fundraiser for his clients. Also, he wasn't human—at least not completely—which made him an excellent fit for politics.

"Stop right there!" I screamed after the fiend. I watched him hightail it around the corner of the eight-foot-high hedge that surrounded the ornamental grounds. Good. The partygoers wouldn't see me take ol'

Hennessey down. Bless the face-melting heat of the Missouri summer—no one inside would venture outside lest common sweat ruin their designer duds.

Unlike my attire, the lobbyist's tailored tuxedo was perfect for hauling ass. The tight red evening dress hugged my knees and made it hard to do much but waddle like a penguin. I tottered around the shrubbery and took an awkward step forward. My heel dipped sideways, and the dewed grass kissed the side of my foot. Ack! My heels! My dearly departed sister Charlotte would be appalled at the treatment of my footwear.

I saw my target just a few feet away from another turn in the boxed hedge. I had scoped out the whole area the day before, so I knew the landscape. I also knew I couldn't catch him before he entered the maze surrounding the marble inlay fountain with its ode to Hennessy himself. Yeah. There was a bronze statue of him holding an American flag in one hand and a champagne bottle in the other.

"I just want to talk," I lied. "Don't you want to make a deal?"

Offering to make a deal to a demon was the equivalent of showering a chocolate addict with truffles. He stopped about twenty feet from me and turned back, his head hitching to one side. "So," he sniffed. "You're the Madder. You don't look like much."

I smoothed my dress, and lifted my chin, and poured on my best Southern drawl. "That's just a mean thing to say, sir. Especially to a lady." My "a"s sounded like "uh"s, and I dropped the "r" in sir. I was pretty proud of the fact that I'd managed to master the non-regional American dialect over the years, but every once in a while, it was fun to pull out the Southern Belle.

The demon in the Hennessey suit snorted, the fear draining from his blue eyes. "Frankly my dear, I don't give a damn."

I loved when they underestimated me. But I hated when they quoted *Gone With the Wind*. I dropped the accent. "I'm not Scarlett, and you're for damn sure not Rhett, so let's cut the shit."

He raised a brow. "You know, now that I see you, I don't know what all the hoopla's about." Curling his lip, he sized me up. "You're kind of doughy."

"That hurts." Actually, it did. I don't care how old you are, women are women everywhere, and none of us want to be thought of as doughy—he might as well have said thick, or hippy, or FAT. Sure, I had curves—some in the wrong places—and my size D breasts were threatening to spill over the top of the borrowed dress, but it didn't give this impostor the right to judge. Especially this skinny, short, pale, and balding imposter about to get his face kicked in.

The "hoop-la" as he called it was the buzz in the underworld about a rogue minion going bat-shit all over demon ass. That rogue would be me, Olivia Madder. Of course, this wasn't the first time I'd been called "the Madder." I've been tracking demons for more than a hundred years and some change. And while I'm not always successful in sending them back to Hell, I had a seventy-seven percent completion rate. Charlotte would've called that bragging, but I called it awesome.

"Tell me about the deal," said Hennessey. "It better be good."

The deal was that I was going to fry him. Now that he had me good and pissed, it was time to teach this uncouth jerk what all the fuss was about. I bent my knee up until I could reach my shoe and nearly fell over as the dress caught on the stiletto. In my struggle to stay upright, the back of the dress ripped at the seam.

Hennessey snorted again. "Had I known that stripping was part of your routine, I might not have been so quick to run."

"Right. You insulted my curves, but now you want to see them?" With the breeze literally at my backside, but infinitely more room to move, I toed off the other shoe so I could get good balance on the balls of my feet.

The demon, undoubtedly baffled, raised a brow. "I don't turn down any opportunity to view the naked female form. Especially given the deficits of my current abode. So, please, do continue bursting out of your clothes."

I flipped him the bird with my free hand, before using my other hand to fling my beautiful red stiletto at him. He seemed startled to be the target of a Frisbee-ing shoe —so you can imagine his surprise when the spiked heel pierced his left eye. I was surprised, too.

I was aiming for his forehead.

A heel between the eyes wouldn't kill the demon, but it would paralyze him long enough for me to work the spell needed to drive him from this plane of existence.

He howled as he toppled onto the well-manicured bluegrass. After a moment, his howls quieted, and he sat up, slack-jawed, and stared at me with his remaining blue eye.

"You rotten bitch." He pointed to the red shoe protruding from his face. "Do you have any idea how hard this body was to come by? And now you've gone and ruined the freaking eyeball."

"If it's any consolation, I didn't mean to hit you in the eye."

"Apology not accepted." He grabbed the heel and struggled to disengage it from his face. "I'm sending you the bill for the blood on my tuxedo."

I leveled my gaze at the demon — oh, sure, he was in human skin, but you can wrap a pile of dog shit in silk, and it's still dog shit, if you catch my meaning — grabbed my other shoe off the ground and tried to walk as menacingly toward my prey as the constricting dress would allow.

I shouldn't have bothered. Hennessey didn't even notice. In fact, he was too busy with shoe extraction to realize I was now standing right beside him.

"What in the name of Moloch is this fucking thing made of?" he yelled.

Iron dipped in holy water and blessed by a white witch, but I wasn't going to tell him that. I held up the other shoe and clicked the steel tip of the heel. A fan of barbs flicked out in a golf ball sized circle. I hit the tip again, and they retracted. The stilettos were my favorite, albeit least comfortable, weapons in my arsenal.

I grabbed the embedded shoe and told the demon, "Hold still."

He tilted his head to the right to give me better access. "Thanks."

Idiot. It was my stylish footwear protruding from his head, and somehow, he thought I was going to help remove it.

"Try not to damage the rest of the face," he ordered. "It's going to be difficult enough to heal the eyeball."

I lowered my head slightly, put on my sweetest smile, and spoke softly. "Don't you worry, honey," I said as I swung my right arm in an arc, "a mangled face is the least of your problems."

"Wait. What?" He looked up at me just in time to realize my intent. Still smiling, I buried the other heel deep into his forehead. *Thud. Crunch. Squish.*

"You suck," the demon mumbled as his left eyelid froze open and he dropped to the ground.

I knelt next to him and, in a gesture taken straight from the offended Southern Belle handbook, I slapped his bloodied face. "That's for your unkind comments about my appearance." I wiped my soiled hands on the demon's shirt. The rusty scent of blood mixed with the fragrance wafting from the colorful flowers planted along the hedges. Well, that was certainly a metaphor of my life —beautiful horror.

All that was left was to send the gored creature back to Hell — once he told me what I wanted to know.

I'd made friends with an Army interrogator back in the nineties. He told me that when they were trying to find Noriega in Panama, they would grab one of his known associates, a person low on the totem pole and easy to find, and make the guy tell them about the next associate, whom they'd go and find, and make that person tell about another one, and so on until they had the location of the tyrant narrowed down.

My focus was less goal-oriented. I only needed to know where to find my next demon. I didn't give a crap about the boss. He was easy to find but impossible to get rid of, so I had to satisfy myself by dispatching all his lackeys. I relied on a website called DemonsAreAmong-Us.com. Its forum was filled with quackery from delusional maniacs who blamed demonic possession for every bad thing in their lives, you know, like their local gas station hiking up the price of super unleaded. Sometimes, though, there would be a post that rang of truth, like the awful one I'd read about the demon Lazul.

Unfortunately, this demon was not Lazul. But he was higher on the pecking order in this particular demonic territory—and he would know where to find the asswipe I really wanted to smite. In Kansas City, Lazul had possessed a young woman who'd committed suicide by overdosing on her antidepressants. She'd been declared dead, and her grieving parents were left alone with the corpse to say their goodbyes. Then the fiend had popped into the corpse, growled obscenities, and yelled, "I am Lazul!" The parents screamed as a demon inhabited their daughter's body. He escaped the hospital before anyone could figure out what was happening.

It was the mom's post, and the particular mentions of rotten-egg smell and glowing red eyes, that sent me after the asshole.

"That's just unsavory," a sweet voice said from behind me, slightly aghast.

"Indeed," another voice agreed, but with more interest than disgust.

"Eww," the final voice mewled. "There's goo leaking from his face."

I rolled my eyes and looked at the three young women now crouched over my shoulder, one brunette, and two blondes — the twins — decked out in full-on bustles and bonnets. Charlotte was more practical than our younger sisters, so her dress was made from pink cotton edged with tiny white flowers. The twins wore pale yellow and lavender chiffon frocks with matching lace gloves and bonnets. Not even death could force my sisters into anything less than their finest attire.

"Go away." I shooed at them. "I'm working."

"Now, Olivia," Char chided, crossing her arms tight against her chest. "Is that any way to greet your sisters?" The way she said sisters, sounded like *sistuhs.*

"Y'all are a distraction I don't need at this moment, Char." I turned the demon's head and held his left eyelid open with my thumb. "Eliza, you probably don't want to watch this."

My youngest sister was squeamish, but mostly because she had an empathic streak a mile wide. Even as a small child on the farm she'd bury dead mice—much to the annoyance of our barn cats that had killed the critters. I imagined that she would've been a social worker or something similar had she lived in this day and age.

I dug my index finger into the demon's unmarred eyeball. "Olivia!" Eliza screeched, her skirts swishing as she skittered backward.

"I told you not to watch."

She buried her face in her hands. The eye gave a little squeak when I breached the surface, and fluid seeped out. It was yucky, but trust me, I've done worse. After a few seconds of digging, I located the bottom of each heel and clicked the barbs closed.

"You used to be the epitome of social standard, Olivia." Charlotte tisked.

"I used to be a lot of things," I said. I glanced at her. "We all did."

Charlotte's gaze fastened on the shoe as I pulled on it. "Careful!" she chided. "It took forever to fix those heels the last time you yanked them out of a vessel's forehead."

"I remember." Considering, I'd done all the work. "I made sure the barbs are closed this time," I told her.

Charlotte had a knack for fixing things. Even with genteel upbringing, Charlotte had always been at home among the farming equipment, fixing broken plows and taking apart tools to figure out how they worked. Poppa, a widowed father, would send us once a week into town to visit with our Aunt Elizabeth, who tried her best to turn us into delicate Belles, but when we were on the farm, Poppa allowed us the freedom of doing more than just house chores. Eliza became an expert on farm animals, pigs, cows, and the like. While Elise, spent all her time reading medical papers she could borrow from Dr. Beauregard Jenkins, a local surgeon, whom she sometimes volunteered with.

Even so, Charlotte couldn't actually get her hands on mechanical objects, but I could, so she walked me through the building and fixing of my demon-hunting weaponry.

Elise, the older of my twin sisters, crouched down for a closer look at the facial damage. I opened the small red clutch and grabbed the three-inch silver rod. I extracted the heel and replaced it with the rod in the center of the demon's forehead. I wiped ocular fluids, brain, and blood from the stilettos onto the demon's shirt, and then slipped them back on my feet.

"I think he has a melanoma on his forehead," Elise said, pointing to a mole on Hennessy's scalp. "It's rough, uneven in color and shape, and I'm sure he never wears sunscreen." She shook her head. "I saw one that looked just like it on Discovery Medicine."

If Elise had been born in modern times, I had no doubt she would be in medical school on her way to being a doctor. I could wish a thousand times my sisters to have different fates, and it wouldn't change a damned thing. Moloch had made sure of that.

I waved at my siblings. "Okay, shoo. Show's over, nothing to see here. Time to go. Last call. Vamoose. Am-scray even."

"You don't have to be rude," said Elise.

"Actually, I do." My sisters could ignore polite, but rude got their attention. Hooking my arms under the demon's armpits, I dragged him around the next hedge. "I'm busy at the moment. I don't have time for niceties. Sorry." Besides, the demon's master—and mine—would be showing up shortly, and I didn't want my sisters anywhere near the foul creature.

All three of them "hmphed" at the same time, then shimmered from sight. Every time they did that, I felt a lightning strike of guilt. The fact that my sisters were ghosts was in no small measure my fault.

I unhooked the chain from the clutch and formed a small circle on the ground next to the paralyzed body. Like the rod, it was made from silver. Demons had what I thought of as a severe allergy to pure silver. Even though I was a minion, the precious metal only felt warm on my skin. It didn't burn.

I'm not evil. Not yet.

I took matches, a votive candle, an orange spice incense cone, a vial of sea salt, a cigarette, and a tiny bell out of the purse. All the items were necessary to the "casting out the boogeyman" spell. Sure, it had another name, a much more complicated, can't hardly get around all the vowels kind of name, but my former demon-hunting partner had deemed it "casting out the boogey-man" and so, that's what we called it.

The familiar heartache threatened to derail my attention. It had been fifty-six years since I'd said goodbye to David Jensen—and yet, it still felt like yesterday. If you're wondering how long it takes to get over that kind of loss, the answer is never.

I poured salt around the silver chain, then I placed the candle and the cone of incense on the north and south edges respectively, struck a match and lit them both. Lifting the demon's hand, I put it inside the loop.

Ugh. I so didn't like this part. I pulled the rod from Hennessey's forehead. The demon howled with rage and pain, his whole body twisting and jerking, except for the trapped hand. His human face contorted in sheer agony. Like I said, silver was bad ju-ju for the damned, and the sea salt made it impossible for the Hellspawn to eject from its host.

That, along with the gaping holes where his eyes used to be, made me shudder inside, a weakness I refused to show to the monsters.

"Hush now," I said, sitting down next to him and trailing my fingers on his brow. "Or the pin goes back in."

"What do you want, Madder?" he asked through gritted teeth.

After all these years, it was still hard to watch human vessels wither under the spell. Sometimes the demons had a shade attached to them, not a ghost exactly — not like my sisters, more like residual energy repeating its traumatic cycle of death over and over. Especially in the newly possessed.

This body didn't have a shade.

It meant this fiend had taken up residence for at least a couple of decades. Hennessy's shade no longer lingered in this realm. "Tell me where I can find Lazul, and I'll let you go." *To Hell.* The Madder wasn't known for mercy to demonkind, and yet, they seem to always believe I'd let them go back to creating havoc for humans.

"I'd rather claw out *your* eyes," the demon rasped.

"Promises, promises." I tapped the hole in his forehead. "Remember who's in charge."

"Bitch!"

"Wow. I hope you don't kiss your mother with that mouth."

"My mother is Sin and Death, and she will feast on your innards while you roast in pits of eternal fire," he screamed, spittle forming in the corners of his lips.

"I know I'm from the South an' all, but I really don't like barbecue." Ugh. He was being stubborn. More stubborn than the average demon who'd roll on another demon to prevent getting a hangnail, let alone the pain of having his hand surrounded by the equivalent of burning pitch.

The body lurched, the empty orbital sockets seemingly staring at me, and Hennessey's voice took on an unnatural tone. "My master will come for you. In the bowels of Hell, you will burn forever. Tenfold, a palsy will fall upon your soul. Tenfold, you will beg for mercy that will never come. Tenfold—"

"Yeah. I got it. Tenfold." I shook my head. "I've heard it all before, asshole." He wasn't going to give me Lazul. From experience, most demons who talked did so in the first minute. This is what I got for trying to go through the slightly higher-ups in the demonic command chain. They weren't as easily broken. Damn it. I really wanted Lazul. Those traumatized parents deserved to put their daughter to rest properly. An empty coffin in the cold ground would be a shitty reminder that her demon-possessed body was running around doing Moloch knew what.

I picked up the cigarette, struck another match, and lit it. Leaning over, I blew a puff of smoke into the demon's face. Cyanide, a by-product of tobacco processing, was a necessary agent in the spell. It didn't take much, and cigarette smoke was the easiest way to transport the minuscule amount of poison, which is why you'd never catch one of Hell's agents smoking.

"Wait. What is that?" His nose twitched as the toxic wisps traveled into his nostrils.

He couldn't see what I was doing, but he realized what was about to happen. Beneath us, the ground shook as the demon fought to release himself from the body before I did. The thing about the boogeyman ritual was that when I used it to expel demons, they got a one-way ticket to Hell. No return trips. It was one of the more satisfying aspects of sending Moloch's lackeys back to the Pit. Time for the *pièce de résistance*. I rang the small bell. Its faint tinkle was reminiscent of a toddler's giggle.

The body instantly stilled.

The demon was gone.

Okay, so most people might have been expecting something spectacular, like out of *Supernatural*. All black smoke, fire, brimstone, explosions, and drama, but nope, just gone.

I'd expected fireworks the first time I cast a demon out of this plane, so I understand the disappointment.

I repacked my clutch, attached the chain before putting it over my shoulder, and got to my feet. I kicked the vessel's thigh. "Take that, Moloch."

Upon mentioning his name, the demon lord burst into existence in front of me.

Fantastic.

Not.

Read More!

ABOUT THE AUTHOR

I am a USA Today Bestselling author who writes paranormal mysteries and romances because I love all things whodunit, Otherworldly, and weird. Also, I wish my pittie, the adorable Kona Princess Warrior, and my beagle, Josie the Incontinent Princess, could talk. Or at least be more like Scooby-Doo and help me unmask villains at the haunted house up the street.

When I'm not writing about mystery-solving were-cougars or the adventures of a hapless psychic living among shapeshifters, I am preyed upon by stray kittens who end up living in my house because I can't say no to those sweet, furry faces. (Someone stop telling them where I live!)

I live in Mid-Missouri with my family and I spend my non-writing time doing really cool stuff...like watching TV and cleaning up dog poop

Follow Renee!

Bookbub

Renee's Rebel Readers FB Group

Newsletter

PARANORMAL MYSTERIES & ROMANCES

BY RENEE GEORGE

Witchin' Impossible Cozy Mysteries

www.witchinimpossible.com
Witchin' Impossible (Book 1)
Rogue Coven (Book 2)
Familiar Protocol (Booke 3)
Mr & Mrs. Shift (Book 4)

Barkside of the Moon Mysteries

www.barksideofthemoonmysteries.com
Pit Perfect Murder (Book 1)
Murder & The Money Pit (Book 2)
The Pit List Murders (Book 3)
Pit & Miss Murder (Book 4)
The Prune Pit Murder (Book 5)

Peculiar Mysteries

www.peculiarmysteries.com
You've Got Tail (Book 1) FREE Download
My Furry Valentine (Book 2)

Thank You For Not Shifting (Book 3)

My Hairy Halloween (Book 4)

In the Midnight Howl (Book 5)

My Peculiar Road Trip (Magic & Mayhem) (Book 6)

Furred Lines (Book7)

My Wolfy Wedding (Book 8)

Who Let The Wolves Out? (Book 9)

My Thanksgiving Faux Paw (Book 10)

Madder Than Hell

www.madder-than-hell.com

Gone With The Minion (Book 1)

Devil On A Hot Tin Roof (Book 2)

A Street Car Named Demonic (Book 3)

Hex Drive

https://www.renee-george.com/hex-drive-series

Hex Me, Baby, One More Time (Book 1)

Oops, I Hexed It Again (Book 2)

I Want Your Hex (Book 3)